# Taming the Billionaire

## Olivia West

# Taming the Billionaire

Published by Olivia West

Copyright © 2019 by Olivia West

ISBN 978-1-07226-859-8

First printing, 2019

www.OliviaWestBooks.com

PRINTED IN THE UNITED STATES OF AMERICA

# Table of Contents

CHAPTER 1 ......................................................... 1

CHAPTER 2 .........................................................10

CHAPTER 3 .........................................................14

CHAPTER 4 .........................................................27

CHAPTER 5 .........................................................37

CHAPTER 6 .........................................................51

CHAPTER 7 .........................................................68

CHAPTER 8 .........................................................79

WHAT TO READ NEXT? ..............................................87

ABOUT OLIVIA WEST ...............................................90

ONE LAST THING.....................................................91

# Chapter 1

"I am strong. I am confident. I will persevere."

Kate looked in the mirror and gave herself a smile as she repeated her mantra while straightening her blazer for the millionth time. Today was the day. Today her future was in the balance and it all hinged on one appointment that had her stomach tied in knots.

"Kate! You are going to be late!"

Kate grabbed her bag and climbed the stairs to the main level of her parents' house to find both of her parents standing at the door expectantly. "Oh, darling, you look very professional. I'm glad you decided to pull your hair back. It makes your face look thinner," her mother said.

"Gee thanks, Mom," Kate grumbled as she walked to the kitchen table where her livelihood, her soap making business, sat waiting. For the last five years she had perfected the craft of making homemade soaps and candles of all types, using her great-grandmother's soap recipe with a few modifications. Her Etsy shop, Pioneer Creations, had made some money but not nearly enough to quit her real job as a barista/accountant at her best friend's bar. Really she was just keeping herself afloat and that was with living in her parents' basement.

"Now make sure you take the blackberry one," her mom was saying as Kate carefully loaded a few candles and soaps into her bag. "That one is your best seller. Oh and the lemon one too."

"I'm sure Katie knows which ones, Laura," her dad interrupted, placing a hand on Kate's shoulder. "We are proud of you, Katie, deal or no deal."

"Thanks, Dad," Kate smiled, hefting the bag onto her shoulder. "Well, wish me luck."

"Oh! Good luck!" her mom said, sniffing into tissue. "Just look at you, all grown up."

"Lord, Mom, I am twenty-eight years old," Kate laughed as she moved to the door. "I've been grown up for a while."

"Well, you are stepping out on your own then," she sniffed as Kate opened the door. "Just remember, you are successful no matter what happens."

Kate shut the door behind her and walked to her car, wishing she had a nicer car to show up to this very important appointment in. It was either her parents' minivan or her four-door clunker and the last image she wanted to project was some soccer mom driving a minivan. She wanted to look professional, though Kate had no idea how to project that past her trusty suit and some confidence. Winging it was about the best idea she had today.

Kate opened the door and put her bag carefully in the front seat, even taking the time to strap it in like it was precious cargo. The last thing she needed to happen was for her dreams to go spilling into the floorboard. She turned the key and the car sputtered to life surprisingly on the first attempt. "That's a good car," Kate crooned, patting the dashboard. Her car, fondly named Betty, had a mind of its own some days, but today it was going to behave.

With a deep breath, Kate pulled out of her parents' driveway and headed toward Wilder Corporation, her mind on what she was going to say. Wilder Corporation was one of the biggest land developers in the state and recently had branched into the hotel business. They were building a lakeside resort not even an hour from Kate's hometown. Kate's best friend, Lilia, had told her that they were looking to incorporate some of the local flavor into this resort, to showcase the area's amenities, and Kate had come up with a crazy notion to showcase her own soaps in the resort.

Turning onto the highway, Kate tapped her fingers on the steering wheel. She was nervous. Her meeting was to be with the owner of Wilder Corporation, James Wilder himself. When she had requested a meeting, she thought she might meet with the marketing guy or even someone even lower than that, but meeting with the head honcho? That was huge. It meant she had to be on top of her game, win him over immediately.

Kate pulled the car into the crowded lot and looked for a close parking spot to squeeze her car into. She had ten minutes before her appointment, enough time to gather all the words she was going to say. Finally she spied one and turned the wheel hard to pull in. The resounding crash of metal on metal took all of the wind out of her sails. Looking over, Kate swallowed hard as she saw the shiny hood of a BMW at her right front tire. Great. Some idiot had tried to take her spot from her! The owner of the car threw open his driver's side door and Kate did the same, hurriedly checking her watch. Nine minutes and counting. She had to make this fast.

"What the hell were you trying to do?"

"Excuse me?" Kate asked coming around the back of her car. Dear Lord, the man was gorgeous. Angry but gorgeous. He was tall, with wavy dark hair that curled just above his expensive suit jacket. Mirrored aviator glasses covered half his face, but she could see his angular face and sensual lips against tanned skin. He was dressed in a sharp grey suit, his blue dress shirt opened at the neck to reveal a delectable patch of skin underneath.

"I was swinging into that parking spot and your clunker of a car about took me out. Lady, that car couldn't fit in there even if you tried."

"I was swinging my clunker into that spot," Kate said defensively, crossing her arms over her chest. "I saw it first."

"The hell you did," he said angrily, shoving a hand through his hair as he looked at the front of his hood. Thank god it wasn't all crunched in but Kate bet that some of his car's baby-blue color was now permanently attached to her passenger side door. "I bet you don't even have insurance."

"My, my, you are nasty," she shot back, all niceties aside. What did he think she was? "Just because I drive a dependable car and not a flashy one doesn't make me any less of a person compared to you."

"A flashy car? Darling, you don't know anything about flashy then. You should see my Lamborghini."

"Wow, that's a horrible pick-up line," Kate laughed. Unbelievable. This guy was so full of himself! She looked down at her watch and saw three minutes left until her appointment. "Shit," she muttered hurrying back to her driver's side. Grabbing an old receipt, Kate hastily scribbled her phone number on the back and thrust it in his direction. "Here. I have got to go but you can call me and we can get your car fixed."

"You're leaving the scene?" he asked harshly. "So you really don't have insurance."

"Geez, dude, get off the insurance crap," she said, pushing the paper at him. "I've got insurance, you arrogant asshole. Take the number or leave it, I don't care. You are making me late for an appointment."

He reached over and snatched the paper out of her hand, giving Kate the green light to climb back in her car and throw it in reverse.

"Hey! Hey!" he shouted, stalking toward her car with an angry expression on his face.

"Not today, dude," she growled, then winced at the sound of metal scraping against metal as she moved Betty out of the way and around the corner after spying another parking spot. Kate spun into it and turned off the engine, grabbing her bag as she sprinted for the building. She was late, because of that asshole, she was late to the most important interview in her entire life. If he cost her this opportunity, she was going to find his BMW and use it as a bumper car. Kate found the elevators and pressed the up button, begging for the elevator to hurry up. Now she was one minute late! Fortunately the doors opened and Kate poured in, hitting the floor button in rapid succession. She had seen once on TV that hitting the buttons on the elevator numerous times did not make it work any faster but she was going to lay on it like her life depended on it today. The doors closed and the elevator mercifully moved upward, giving Kate only a minute to compose herself. She could do this provided that the head of the company would still see her. Maybe she could explain what happened to her in the parking lot and he would sympathize. Yes, she would play to his sympathy immediately.

The doors opened and she rushed out, nearly sprinting to the receptionist desk. "I-I am here to see Mr. Wilder."

The blonde receptionist looked up at her, her eyes narrowing at the sound of Kate huffing and puffing in her ear. "Excuse me?"

"Kate Hensley to see Mr. Wilder. I have a two o'clock with him."

"You're late, Ms. Hensley."

"Oh come on, it's one minute," Kate huffed, glaring at the woman. "You can take a minute off my time with him then."

"You are two minutes late," the woman replied, her long red nails clicking on her computer. "Take a seat and I will see if *Mr. Wilder* still wants to meet with you."

Kate smiled sweetly and took a seat on the sofa near the desk, hoping that she wasn't as sweaty as she felt. First the nasty man in the parking lot and now Ms. Queen Bitch herself. Great, her day was getting better by the moment. "Focus, Kate," she whispered to herself, taking in a deep breath and letting it out. Nothing else mattered except getting into that office and pitching her idea. If she didn't even make it in there, well, she failed all the way around.

She waited ten minutes before the receptionist even looked in her direction, the look on the blonde's face not friendly at all. "Mr. Wilder says he can still meet with you, Ms. Hensley. Please go on in."

"Thank you," Kate said, ignoring the disdain in the receptionist's voice as she stood and walked through the door. The office was massive, with a large desk and plush carpeting that made Kate want to take off her sturdy shoes and sink her toes in it. The chair was spun toward the windows so she couldn't see Mr. Wilder but Kate forced a smile anyway as she sat on one of the chairs in front of the desk. Here goes nothing. "Mr. Wilder, I'm Kate Hensley. I've got a product that I think you will be interested in for your new resort. It's locally made with elements from our fair state and handcrafted by myself." Kate took a deep breath and waited for him to say something, to turn around and applaud her opening statement. When he didn't she scrambled to continue. "I have a few samples of both my soap and my candles that could potentially not only stock the rooms but also be available for sale in the gift shop. My inventory stays full so there is no concern of running out. I am trying new concoctions every day so there is always a new product to try out." She then sat back, pleased with her spiel. "I am persistent, Mr. Wilder, and driven to succeed. I want to make your resort as successful as I can."

"So you are persistent, Ms. Hensley?"

"I am, sir," Kate said slowly, her grin fading into a look of surprise and shock as the chair spun around.

"You!"

# Chapter 2

Mr. BMW Asshole himself was staring back at her, his gaze narrowed. She could see that his eyes were a deep brown with gold flecks in them. "You aren't James Wilder," she accused, her own eyes narrowing. Was this some sick joke?

"I am not," he admitted, leaning on the desk with his elbows. "I am Luke Wilder, the youngest son of James Wilder." She watched aghast as he coolly assessed her from head to toe, no doubt sizing her up for a pair of handcuffs. She had left the scene of an accident, hadn't she? What did the police do to people who were accident skippers? The son. Great. There was no way in hell she was going to get this now. Daddy probably already knew she had dented pretty boy's car and had allowed him to handle his dirty work. Kate's stomach plummeted as she thought of her high hopes, the way her parents were going to react at their daughter failing to reel in the big fish.

"I am the marketing CEO of my father's company," he continued, oblivious to her pity party. "I approve all aspects of product and advertisement."

Kate bit her tongue against a snarky retort and nodded, hoping that her face wasn't projecting what she was feeling at the moment. What she really wanted to do was roll her eyes and do a "woohoo" at the way that he had enunciated his job title but that wouldn't be very professional of her. Actually there was nothing in her mind that seemed to be very professional at the moment. Instead she straightened her shoulders and hoped that her voice sounded light and unaffected.

"I can certainly meet the needs of your father's new resort, Mr. Wilder. I believe my products will bring the essence of what the local flavor is. Your customers will have the very best fragrances from around the state."

"What about volume, Ms. Hensley? You are, what, a one-woman show? I have pulled your accounts from the online dealings you have been doing. You average about two to three sales a month. Our resort will easily handle over a thousand or more vacationers a month."

"I am a one-woman show," she replied, grinding her teeth at his tone of voice. This man was cold and calculating, his very demeanor telling her that he didn't approve of her or her business. "But I am also very good with my products. I can ensure you that I will be more than capable to handle the workload."

He sighed and laid down the paper he had been holding. "Ms. Hensley, what business knowledge do you have? What degree do you hold? A small online store with very little profit does not make me all warm and fuzzy on the inside. It's obvious that you have no experience."

"You are going to hold that against me?" she blurted out, surprised. "Mr. Wilder, I know we started off on the wrong foot this morning but that is no reason to pick me apart. Surely a businessman like you can see the potential in this product. It's exactly what your father is looking for." How dare he? Just because she didn't have her own Harvard degree in business didn't mean that she hadn't scrimped and clawed her way to making her business successful! She doubted anything would make him warm and fuzzy on the inside. He was as hard as one of her bars of soap and right now, she wanted to chunk it at his head. Maybe he would see the potential then. A sniggle of laughter escaped her and his eyes narrowed even more. Great.

"I will leave my products here in case you are inclined to try them," she forced out, placing her bag on the desk as she stood. "I appreciate your time, Mr. Wilder." It was time to exit before this got any worse. It was very clear to her that he didn't care about her soaps or about launching them in the resort. She had lost it before she really ever had a chance.

Kate turned on her heel and headed to the door, the anger building. He had judged her solely because she had no experience, not to mention the accident this morning. Or was it her mouth or her appearance? Was it the combination of everything that made Kate?

"I'm sorry, Mr. Wilder," she blurted out, turning around to look at him still scowling at her. "I do not have a college education nor do I have a multimillion-dollar business. I don't have tons of employees or even a factory that you can watch churn out the product. What I do have is determination and heart. I have what every struggling business person starts out with. I am sure somewhere in your family's existence there was someone like me who built this empire from the ground up. I just hate that you can't relate to the fact that we don't all come from money nowadays." She then turned around and walked out of the door.

# Chapter 3

"You didn't really say that, did you?"

"I did," Kate swallowed, peeling the label from her beer bottle. "I said all of that and more but the way he was so condescending I couldn't help it."

Lilia whistled low as she wiped the scarred wooden bar top, her blonde hair falling about her face with every motion. "Geez, he must really be a prick then. I haven't met him personally, but I have heard rumors that old man Wilder himself plucked him from another one of his companies in the city and planted him here. Maybe that's why he's so angry."

"It's either that or because I scratched his precious car," Kate muttered. If he filed that claim her insurance was going to go through the roof.

"Well, if he doesn't accept your offer, he's an idiot," Lilia said as she moved away. Kate watched her friend help another patron and sighed, knowing that she was right. So what if Luke Wilder didn't want to take a chance on her? There were plenty of other places that she could target. Half of the town sold her soaps anyway so it was just a matter of time before someone noticed them and she would be a success overnight. Then the Wilders would be begging for her products.

Kate looked around the semi-crowded bar, thinking of how Lilia had struggled in her first year. She had inherited it from her uncle and had known nothing about running a business like this but in the last two years, her friend's career had started to turn a corner. Coyotes was really starting to turn a profit and Kate could see the upswing in patronage in the last year. It was becoming a hot spot for the locals and Lilia had some great dreams of expanding what the bar had to offer. It was Kate's job to ensure that her friend still continued to make money, even though she didn't have a degree to prove that she knew all about money.

Snorting, Kate finished off her beer and resumed peeling the label on the beer bottle. So what if she hadn't finished her accounting degree? Her knack for numbers had helped out her friend greatly when she couldn't afford to hire staff and what Kate knew about the business side of the world had helped her launch her own business. So what if it hadn't starting spouting out millions of dollars? Small profits would eventually turn into bigger ones, which was what she had hoped would happen today. If only Luke Wilder hadn't held her dreams in his hand and crushed them before she really got started.

"Oh my god, that is a hot piece if I've ever seen one! Kate, you have got to check out the ass on that one."

Smirking at the sound of Lilia's hushed voice, Kate turned around and admired the rear view along with every other woman in the bar. Lilia was right, the man did have a great rear end, encased in a pair of faded jeans and topped with a green shirt. From her vantage point, she could make out the broad shoulders under his tee. "Can you imagine what he looks like from the front?"

"Our luck he is missing a vital piece of his face or has a unibrow," Lilia sighed, resting her chin on her upturned palm. "But the unibrow could be fixed quickly. Who do you think he is?"

Kate shrugged as she watched him talk on his cell phone near the door, wondering herself. "I don't know, maybe passing through? He would be a perfect target for you, my friend. It's been like what, two years?"

"Hell, you haven't done any better," Lilia said, pushing at Kate's shoulder. "What was your last one, John?"

Kate's heart did a familiar ache and she forced the ache back into its hiding hole and slammed that door shut, not wanting to relive those feelings ever again. John was the reason she was living in her parents' basement. She had moved out of their rented townhouse after she caught him sexting with a coworker. They had dated two years and she had been devastated at his betrayal. "So what," she forced out with a shrug. "I've been busy with my soaps."

"Well, the soaps won't keep you warm at night," Lilia remarked with a wry smile. "But he would; probably day and night if I had to guess. Oh look, he's turning around! Please be hot, please be hot."

Kate smirked as she watched the stranger turn around, her smirk turning to a sour frown as she recognized his features. Crap. "Don't get too excited, Lilia. His looks are very deceiving."

"Wait, that's Luke Wilder? You didn't tell me he was hot!"

"Lilia!" Kate hissed, turning her attention back to her friend, who was fanning herself with her hand. "It shouldn't matter, he's an asshole."

"He might be that but he's still hot. Even you have to admit that one."

"Fine, he looks pretty good," Kate forced out, slinking low on her stool. So what. He still was mean.

"Oh my god, he's coming this way!"

"What, no," Kate scrambled to get out of her seat. She wasn't going to make nice conversation with him, not after the way he treated her today!

"A beer, please."

Crap, it was too late. The scent of spicy cherries assaulted her senses as he took the stool next to her.

Lilia nodded and moved away while Kate tried to look everywhere but at him. Fate had to be against her today.

"Ms. Hensley?"

"Mr. Wilder," she sighed, turning toward him. "What a surprise." He looked less formidable in casual clothes, though it didn't dim his hotness. His dark hair was windblown from being outside, his gold-flecked eyes showing surprise as he looked at her. Up close she could see the stubble on his tanned cheeks.

"A surprise indeed," he echoed as Lilia set the bottle in front him. "She looks like she needs a refill. Put it on my tab."

"No, you don't have to do that," Kate quickly said, shooting a glaring look at Lilia. "I can handle my own tab." She didn't want to owe him anything. Hell, she probably already owed him hundreds to fix his car.

In the end, her friend betrayed her. "Another beer coming up," Lilia replied with a wink as she moved toward the cooler behind the bar. Kate wanted to throw her bottle at her friend's retreating form but she refrained and focused on the man she hated more instead. "Thanks."

"It's the least I could do," he said with a sigh, running his hand though his hair roughly. By the state of his hair, she imagined he did that quite often.

"Listen, I might have been a bit harsh with you earlier."

Kate did a double take as his words sank in, not believing that those words had come out of his mouth. "You're joking, right?"

"I wasn't having the best of days," he frowned, looking down at the beer in his hands. "And I took it out on you unfairly."

"Um, okay," Kate replied, unsure if she was on *Candid Camera* or not. She was surprised that he was apologizing to her and was making her feel perhaps a little guilty that she had automatically thought the worst of him. "Well, thanks for the beer. I've got to go."

"Here's your beer, Kate!" Lilia said with a smile as she looked at Luke. "Welcome to Coyotes. I'm Lilia the fearless owner of this establishment. If you need anything at all, Kate can help you, can't you, Kate?"

"I was just about to leave," Kate muttered grabbing the bottle.

"I'm Luke Wilder," he said, holding out his hand. Lilia giggled as she shook it while Kate rolled her eyes, knowing that her friend was no longer on her side. It wasn't fair, this wasn't the Luke she had met earlier. "Nice to meet you, Luke. Where are you from?"

"Chicago until yesterday," he said, releasing Lilia's hand. "I've been relocated."

Chicago. No wonder he was in such a foul mood. Their town of Haper didn't offer anywhere near as much as Chicago would. Sure they were close to an interstate and had a pretty awesome lake, but that was about it. Everything else was more on the "small town you never leave" side. She had been born and raised here as well as many generations of her family before her.

"Well, I will leave you to conversation then," Lilia was saying with a small wave Kate's way. "Make sure you take him upstairs to try out the pool tables. I just had them renovated."

"So this is her bar?"

"What? You think she can't run her business either?" Kate shot out. "What's your problem?"

"I was going to say how impressed I was about that," he replied evenly, a hint of a smile on his face. Gah, he had dimples. She loved dimples! "I guess I really made a bad impression today."

"I guess you did," she said softly, some of the anger toward him dissipating. Maybe he really was a decent guy and she had misjudged him. Hadn't she had some bad days in her past? "It's fine really. I'm sorry for my comments and laying into you." She then stuck out her hand toward him sheepishly. "Kate Hensley."

"Luke Wilder," he said, sliding his hand into hers. His grip was firm, his touch warm and Kate felt the first stirrings of butterflies in her stomach. "Nice to meet you, Kate. I hear that you are an up-and-coming entrepreneur?"

"And I hear you are some hotshot marketing executive," she countered with a laugh as he let go of her hand. "With a dinged-up BMW."

"Good thing I drove the Lambo tonight then," he winked and Kate's breath caught. Oh my. Lilia was right. He was hot when she didn't want to ping him in the head with her soaps. He was probably the hottest guy that she had ever talked to for longer than five minutes. Hot guys didn't exactly step into her path very often. She was not exactly a tall blonde with a tight body after all. She was, well, a few pounds over what she should be and her dark hair and eyes never really stood out in the crowd. Her chest was more than a handful unless you were a giant and tended to garner unwanted attention during those really late, really drunk nights Lilia liked to make her cover at the bar. All in all, she was the complete opposite of what Mr. Luke Wilder was probably used to.

"So does that line really work?" she finally asked.

"It does when I take them for a ride in it," he laughed, taking a swig of his beer. Kate had never wanted to be a beer bottle so badly. What had happened? She had gone from hating the man to wanting to lick the underside of his chin in like five minutes! "Would you like to go for a ride, Kate?"

"I, um, I have seen your driving and it stinks," she forced out, her face red at the way her mind was processing his words. The thought of him under her made her hot and bothered all at once. Had he really meant riding in the car or was there an undertone with his comment? Was she way overthinking the entire comment? Her mind was in a whirlwind right now at everything that had happened between the two of them in a very short timeframe.

"I would say the same about yours, Kate," he grinned. "We will agree to disagree on that subject."

"Agreed," she said, forcing all notions of riding Luke out of her mind. This was casual conversation, not some down and dirty hookup. She needed to tone it down. "So big-town guy stuck in a small town, that probably isn't your cup of tea."

"I would have to say that you are correct on that," Luke sighed, downing his beer and signaling for another. The bar area was really starting to fill up as the patrons of Haper started their Friday night shenanigans. Normally Kate was working the bar as well, but Lilia had given her the day off with the hopes of celebrating her success later. Now it was just a wasted night that Kate wouldn't make money on. Instead she was spending her time with the man who had just shut down her dreams. Well, maybe that was a little harsh. He hadn't given his verdict yet. "I miss the traffic, the sights and sounds of the city at night. I miss the variety."

"I've never been to a big city," Kate admitted, feeling very not worldly at the moment. "Well, really I haven't even been over the state line."

"Seriously?" Luke asked, astounded. "Not even to Florida or Vegas or to the west coast?"

"Not even," she said, thinking about how pathetic it was. She was twenty-eight and never had been out to see the world. She had been so busy trying to be successful in her little company and in her personal life that it never occurred to her how much she was missing out. Not anymore, she decided silently. If she could wrangle this deal then she was going to find herself some little apartment that didn't cost much and take some of the money and schedule a trip somewhere. Maybe New York or Disney World. "I'm sure you have traveled a great deal."

"A bit," he shrugged, like it wasn't a big deal. "Last summer I spent some time in Spain picking up some authentic pieces for our hotel in Florida."

"So what is your job anyway?" Kate asked as a local band started up in the far corner of the room. "Is it marketing or shopping?"

"A little bit of this and that.," Luke grinned, pushing off his barstool. "Didn't your friend say something about pool tables?"

"Um, sure, this way," Kate said. She got off her stool and led him up the stairs into the loft that overlooked the space below. Since the live music had started the loft was empty, the tables open and ready for play. "Do you play pool?"

"I'm not so bad," Luke replied, stretching his arms over his head. Kate caught a glimpse of a tanned, flat stomach and looked away, her heart racing. Wow, she hadn't seen anything like that live and in person in a while. Adjusting her own shirt so she didn't flash him her stomach, Kate placed the balls on the table and grabbed the rack nervously. She wasn't very good at pool, never really getting down the concept that the stick was to hit the ball though she and Lilia had attempted to play many nights. Placing the balls like she remembered, Kate positioned them just right and removed the rack, giving Luke a smile as she handed him a pool stick. "Why don't you go first?"

"Okay," he said positioning himself to break. Kate's cheeks flamed as she took in the view of his lean body draped over the pool table. She was trying to remember what in the world she was trying to accomplish by hanging out with him. Should she be bringing up her company again, pitching her idea or should she just relax and enjoy herself? Guys like him didn't normally hang out with girls like her. Luke expertly sent the cue ball crashing into the racked balls and they scurried for the pockets. "I'm calling solids," he announced as he aimed for the solid red ball. Kate just nodded as he shot that one in and then another before finally missing one. It was her turn. Her hands trembling, Kate positioned herself across the table, ignoring the way Luke's eyebrow arched as she gripped the pool stick in her hands. Just one ball at a time, she pleaded to herself as she pulled the stick back and thrust it forward at the cue ball. To her horror the ball skipped over the table and right at Luke, hitting him in a vital place before he went down to the floor.

"Oh my god," she breathed as she dropped the stick and rushed to his side. He was grimacing in pain. "Are you okay?"

"Hell," he forced out, cupping himself as he lay in the fetal position on the floor. Kate bit her lip as she tried to figure out what to do. Ice, he needed ice. Taking the stairs two at a time, she hurried over to the bar and grabbed a clean rag, then threw ice from the open cooler in it.

"Kate? What's going on? What are you doing?"

"I, I did something horrible," she said as she tied up the rag tightly and looked at Lilia. "I hit him in you know where with a pool ball."

"Oh dear," Lilia said, looking up at the loft. "I said to play pool, not try to kill him with it. Go! I just hope he doesn't sue."

Kate hurried back up the stairs and found Luke in a semi-standing position, hunched over the pool table with his hands on his face. "Here," she said breathlessly, shoving the rag at him. "This ice should help."

He looked up and she grimaced, seeing the pain in his eyes. "I'm so sorry. I didn't mean to do that."

"It's fine," he said tightly, straightening. "I think I am going to call it a night." Kate watched as he limped over to the stairs and sighed, realizing that she probably had just maimed a smoking guy for life and lost the deal. Great, her life was getting better and better by the minute.

# Chapter 4

"I'm being so stupid for this. He's not going to want to see my face," Kate thought as she squared her shoulders and looked up at the townhouse with apprehension, her feet wanting to run in the opposite direction. The smell of the colorful bouquet tickled her nose and she suppressed the urge to sneeze while wondering if men liked to get flowers. Probably not but she couldn't think of anything else to get him at the moment. It wasn't like they sold "I'm sorry I hit you in the balls" cards at the drugstore. She had called in a favor to a realtor friend of hers and was able to find the townhouse that Luke was renting under the Wilder Corporation name. It was in a nice subdivision known for its beautiful homes and way beyond anything Kate could afford currently. She didn't know what had possessed her to even think of this, but she felt really, really bad about what had happened last night and wanted to apologize in person. It had nothing to do with the pending deal really, but more along the lines of how much she had actually enjoyed hanging out with him last night. A part of her couldn't help but think of what might had happened if she hadn't been so horrible at pool.

With a sigh she marched up to the door and rang the doorbell, shifting the vase of flowers in her arms. If he didn't answer she would just leave them on the doorstep and hope that he appreciated the thought at least. Maybe she should have done that to begin with. What if he shut the door in her face? Wouldn't that be ten times worse? Setting the vase on the steps, Kate decided that she would rather not apologize as she headed back down the stairs to the safety of her car.

"Kate?"

Too late, she was so busted. With a deep breath, she turned around to find Luke holding the vase of flowers like they were going to attack him, surprise on his face. "Um, hi Luke. I just wanted to apologize for last night and see if you were okay. I see that you are upright and moving so I will just leave now."

"You brought me flowers?"

"I, yes," she said sheepishly. "I didn't know what kind of alcohol you preferred and the flowers could be left. The alcohol, well it might not have lasted long on your doorstep given that someone might help themselves to the free stuff." Great, she was rambling on now. He must think she was such a dork.

Instead of staring at her he threw his head back and laughed. "Kate, you are full of surprises."

"So I have been told," she mumbled. "Enjoy the flowers. I hope that you can accept my apology."

"Oh, I am not accepting your apology just yet," he said, some of the laughter fading from his face. "Mere flowers aren't going to solve this one."

"I, um, okay," Kate stuttered, her heart pounding at what he might want her to do. It wasn't like she had cut off a finger or anything. Oh god, had she maimed him in some way? Was she going to have to add a hospital bill on top of the insurance claim she already owed him?

"I want you to attend a dinner with me tonight."

"I, what?" she sputtered, looking at him for any hint of joking on his face. Nope, dead serious. That was her punishment? Was he going to embarrass her, make her pay for the incidents she had already caused him?

"Dinner, with me tonight," he repeated, arching an eyebrow. "I won't accept your apology unless you do."

"This is so weird," Kate muttered looking at him. "Then we will be even?"

"Maybe not even but I will be able to let this go," he smiled, turning. "I will pick you up at five, Kate. You have three hours." He then handed her his phone, the map search already open. "Put in your address."

"Why should I?" she asked hesitantly, looking down at the sleek device.

"You want this over with, right?" he asked, pushing the phone at her. "Come on, it's just dinner."

Kate swallowed the retort she was itching to give him and typed in her parents' address before she changed her mind. This was going to be extremely awkward tonight given their short history with each other.

"Thank you," he grinned and shut the door. Kate stood there for a moment, wondering what the heck had just happened. Dinner? Really? That was it? Lilia wasn't going to believe any of this.

***

"I have nothing to wear! What do you wear when you don't even know where you are going?"

Kate moaned into the phone as she threw a pair of jeans across the room and sank onto the bed in despair. She had thirty minutes before Luke arrived and she was still clad in her bra and underwear.

"Just wear something flirty, not too slutty though. You don't want to look desperate, Kate."

"I am desperate," Kate replied, pushing off the bed to go back to her closet. "I don't own anything slutty, Lilia. Isn't that your closet?

"Oh yeah," Lilia laughed. "Maybe you should have come and shopped in my closet then."

Kate thought about her slim, blonde friend and laughed, thinking that one boob wouldn't fit into one of Lilia's shirts. "Yeah, right. Alright, I have to go. I can't go naked."

"Call me tomorrow and don't leave out the details," Lilia sang. "This is epic, Kate. I think he really likes you."

"And I think you are crazy, right behind him," Kate said as she pressed end and threw the phone on the bed. She had to find something to wear. Pushing the hangers back and forth, Kate finally pulled out a dress she had bought years ago but never wore. It was a pretty teal color, with a V-neck and cap sleeves that would be perfect for the balmy night. The bottom was a swing skirt style and fell at a comfortable length just below the knee. It wasn't too dressy, but dressy enough in case he took her somewhere fancy. She could even bowl in it if that was his plan. She hoped he would steer clear of any pool table balls for a while.

With a sigh Kate slid the dress over her head and straightened it around her body, loving the feel of the soft material against her skin. For some strange reason she had plucked, shaved, and pulled out her sexiest undergarments for tonight. It had been quite a while since she had been out that didn't involve Coyotes and the thought of being on Luke's arm had her insides in a tight ball. "This is just dinner," she reminded herself as she looked in the mirror, critiquing her look. Her hair was down and after a load of product, the waves were almost perfect in her long dark hair with just a hint of highlights. Her makeup was pretty good too and in this dress, Kate almost felt like a million bucks.

"Kate! Someone is here to see you!"

"Oh no," Kate moaned as she thought of Luke being grilled by her parents. It was a fate worse than death. Finding a perfect pair of sandals, Kate threw them on and grabbed both her bag and fringed shawl off her bed before climbing the steps up to the main level. She just hoped that her mom didn't ask too many questions before she could save Luke from her mom's never-ending questions, like what his last name was. She hadn't told them that she was going out with a Wilder. Turning the corner, Kate skidded to a stop as she saw Luke in the doorway. He looked good enough to eat, a suit draping his form complete with a steel-blue dress shirt underneath, unbuttoned at the throat. She had picked very well with her clothing selection to complement his style tonight. For that, she was very, very glad.

"Oh, you look so beautiful. You both look so beautiful! Harold, where is my camera?"

"I think it's in the bedroom, Laura," her father grumbled as Kate watched Luke's easy smile grow wider.

"I will be right back," her mom said as she disappeared around the corner in search of her offending camera.

"Go, while you have a chance," her father urged, shooing them both toward the door. "Have fun."

"Thanks, Dad," Kate smiled gratefully as Luke opened the front door. "Oh god, you really do have one."

"I told you," Luke said as he led her to a gleaming yellow Lamborghini in her parents' driveway, right behind Kate's clunker. "Get in."

Kate tried to keep her mouth closed as she walked carefully around the car and pulled on the handle, the door sliding up instead of out. Geez, that car had to cost more than her parents' house and cars combined! Carefully she slid into the supple leather seat and allowed Luke to pull down the door, not wanting to touch anything lest she scratch something. Luke climbed in and gunned the engine, maneuvering the car out of the drive with ease. Kate didn't think she had ever seen anything sexier than him behind the wheel of an outrageously expensive car and swallowed hard. She was in way over her head. Lilia was going to freak out. "I'm sorry about my mom. She gets really excited when I go out." Oh great, now she sounded like she was a hermit whose dating game sucked! Never mind, her dating game did suck and suck royally.

"It's fine. Your parents were very nice," Luke replied as he eased the car onto the highway. "They care about you. There's nothing wrong with that."

Kate smiled as she leaned back, keeping her hands clutched tightly around her bag. "So do you have a Porsche as well?"

"I do not," he grinned, his gorgeous dimple appearing and sending Kate into a state of overheating. "My brother Josh does, several of them in fact. He races them on occasion. I prefer the sleekness myself."

"It's a gorgeous car," Kate said, clearing her throat as he pulled into the parking lot of the small county airport. This was where they were going? She hadn't been to the airport since the air show last year but unless they had secretly installed a restaurant, her memory didn't conjure up a restaurant or anything to that effect. Luke parked the car and cut the engine, looking over at her. "I know what you are thinking, Kate. I failed to mention we needed to fly to the dinner."

"Are you serious?" she blurted out. Fly? That was a very foreign word to her. "Are you pulling my chain or something?"

"Come on, Kate," he laughed as he climbed out of the car. Kate waited until he threw open her door before she struggled out of the low-sitting car, accepting his hand for help. The warmth of his touch sent her head reeling and her mind blanked as she stood before him, so close that she was enveloped in his spicy scent. "Do you trust me?"

Kate looked at him, marveling at the tiny gold flecks in his deep brown eyes and the small amount of space between their bodies. She found herself wanting to throw herself at him just to see what he would do. Her feelings were so different than what she had experienced with John, a whole new sensation that she wasn't quite sure of what to do with. Could she trust him? Did she want to? "For now," she finally said, forcing herself to pull her hand out of his grasp and step back. She didn't want to get involved with him, not on this level. It was a road to heartbreak, this one was.

"That's good enough," he said, motioning toward the hangar. "This way."

Kate followed him through the fence and to the hangar with some trepidation, her stomach in more knots than earlier. Flying. The very thought scared her half to death. Was he going to pilot the plane? Was it a plane or a helicopter or hot-air balloon? Okay, maybe not the balloon but either way her body was screaming that it wasn't a good idea. How many planes crashed and burned daily?

"Kate, this is Lewis. He will be our pilot tonight. Lewis, Kate."

Kate looked up to find a smiling man in a pilot's uniform holding out his hand and took it. "Nice to meet you, Kate. I hope this flight is one of your best yet."

"I don't have anything to compare it with," she admitted softly as she dropped her hand. Lewis's eyes widened but he said nothing and turned back to the jet behind him, climbing the stairs and disappearing inside.

"You've never flown before?"

"Guilty as charged," she replied, turning toward Luke. "I told you, small-town girl, small-town world. Flying isn't a necessity." How he must think of her!

Instead of laughing, he reached out and touched a wayward strand of her hair, feeling it between his fingers. "I think you are going to enjoy this night just as much as I will, Kate."

"I hope so," she squeaked out as he dropped his hand. She just hoped she didn't embarrass herself or injure him further. Or cause the plane to crash. That was something she definitely couldn't cover.

# Chapter 5

"Are you freaking serious?! I can't believe it. We were just talking about it last night."

Luke chuckled as he leaned back in the leather chair, his eyes alight with laughter. "See? Aren't you glad you accepted?"

Kate nearly squealed in glee as she threw up the shade on the window next to her, nearly beside herself as she glimpsed the New York skyline in the setting sun. They were going to New York! For an hour she had kept conversation light while the destination had been a burning question in her mind. When she had drummed up enough courage to ask, she had been totally shocked by the answer. Flying wasn't too bad, she had decided, the takeoff a little rough but it had been pretty smooth ever since and now a whole new nervousness was setting in. Lilia was definitely not going to believe this! "I can't believe this."

"Well, I hope it is everything you hoped it would be," he said smoothly, draining his glass of whiskey before setting it aside. She had been too nervous to drink and the attendant had still produced a glass of water that was sitting untouched in her armrest. Kate had wanted nothing to ruin this experience and alcohol was definitely out of the picture for as long as she could tonight. New York! She had so much she wanted to ask Luke, so much she would like to see but this wasn't a tourist trip. Giving him a megawatt smile, she forced herself to tamp down the excitement as she smoothed her skirt with her hands. "Thank you."

"For what?" he asked as the plane started its descent.

"For taking me here tonight," she answered. "You could have just taken me to the Italian place around the corner but instead, this is craziness, you know that?"

"There's a hidden agenda," he said, rubbing the back of his neck with his hand. "This is a gala thrown by my family, Kate. I probably should have told you sooner."

"I, well, that's okay too," she swallowed, her excitement dimming. So they weren't going on a date, but more like he needed a date for this gala thing. She was a little bummed at the thought. They wouldn't be alone, but surrounded by people that she had nothing in common with. She would have to pretend that she fit in. He was going to make her pay dearly. What if she wasn't dressed appropriately?

"You look gorgeous by the way," Luke said gently as the plane jostled onto the runway. Kate's head snapped up to look at him, surprise forming on her face. "I mean it, Kate. I couldn't ask for a better-looking date."

Okay, well she would take that and eat it up! Maybe this wasn't going to be so bad after all.

***

It wasn't bad, it was worse. They had arrived to a crowded ballroom inside the Waldorf Astoria, a ritzy hotel in midtown Manhattan. Kate had marveled at the sights and sounds of a busy city, the traffic incredible compared to what she was used to back home. The entire city was bright with lights everywhere she looked, the buildings towering into the sky and beyond. She wanted to get out and walk around, to dwell on the fact that she, Kate Hensley from Podunk Haper, was in New York City with a gorgeous man at her side. Unfortunately that was not what they were here for and from the first moment they had stepped inside the ballroom, Kate had felt way out of place. Everywhere she looked she saw money, from the expensive dresses to the glittering jewels that sparkled in the dim lighting. There was champagne being passed out by waiters as they had walked in and Kate had taken one for appearance, though she hadn't touched it. The room was full of the droning of conversation and soft piano music as people drifted from place to place with a smile, frown, or laugh. Thankfully Luke hadn't left her side, but at every turn he was being stopped. She had stood quietly behind him, her hands clasped around her evening bag with a frozen smile pasted on her lips for the last hour. She would rather be anywhere than here.

"You look bored stiff."

Surprised, Kate turned to find a tall, dark-haired man lounging against the wall next to her, his gold-flecked eyes shockingly familiar. "Excuse me?"

"You know, like you would rather be at the dentist than here," he grinned, pushing away from the wall to stand next to her. "My brother is an idiot for dragging you here."

"Y-your brother?" she stammered, looking ahead to find Luke swallowed up by the pressing crowd. "Josh with the Porsches?"

"Well, I prefer Josh the black sheep car-racing idiot," he laughed aloud, grabbing her elbow as he steered them through the crowd. "But that will do as well. Josh Wilder at your service."

"Kate Hensley," she forced out. "Where are you taking me? I really should find Luke."

Josh stopped and turned toward her, his eyes twinkling mischievously as he stared down at her. He was just as handsome as his brother, though his hair was all over his head and brushing the collar of his dress shirt. He was jacketless, his pants wrinkled like he had slept in them. This was a far cry from the put-together Luke she had been getting used to. "You look like a beer girl, Kate." Kate looked at the champagne glass still full in her hand and blushed as he plucked it out, setting it on a tray as it passed. "Tell me I am wrong, go ahead."

"You aren't wrong," she said softly. He grinned warmly and proffered his arm to her. "I know where there is excellent beer. Don't you worry about my brother. He will find us soon enough." Against her better judgment, Kate took his arm and he escorted her to the far corner of the room, where a lone table was sitting empty near the exit. "Have a seat, Kate. I will be right back."

Kate sat and pulled her bag into her lap. She was surprised when Josh reappeared just as quickly as he had disappeared, two cold beer bottles in his hands. "Wow. You must have a cooler nearby."

"I do actually, stocked full for a night like this," he laughed, handing her one of the bottles as he sat in the chair next to her. "I hate champagne. It's too stuffy. It drives my family crazy when I drag my cooler into their event."

"You're joking, right?" Kate giggled, taking a swig of the beer. God, it was good.

"I'm not," he said, waggling his eyebrows at her. "Black sheep, remember? It wouldn't be a party unless I did drag my cooler along."

Kate giggled louder and then ducked her head as she drew looks her way. She was feeling way too comfortable with this brother of Luke's. "Why even come then?" she asked as he took a healthy swallow himself.

"You're joking, right?" he echoed then smiled. "There is no declining these events. When your family is ponying up millions of dollars to some charity or campaign function you must make an appearance. Wilder rules." He then sighed, his smile dimming. "I'm missing an important race because of this."

Kate didn't say anything but her heart went out to him. It was obvious racing was important to him by the look on his face. She was missing out on the experience of a lifetime in New York so she could relate. What had made Luke drag her to this? To torture her? "So you and my baby brother," Josh was saying. "No offense but you are different than his last girlfriend. It looks like he has finally garnered some taste in his picks."

Kate nearly spit out a whole mouthful of beer, but managed to swallow it down as she set her bottle gently on the table. "I'm not his girlfriend by any stretch of the imagination but I think you just gave me a compliment anyway so thanks."

"I did and you must be pretty important for him to bring you here," Josh replied with a wink.

Kate kept her smile but inside her thoughts were screaming with questions. What had his last girlfriend looked like? "He only brought me here because I sent a pool ball into his vital parts last night," she said finally.

Josh's eyes grew wide and he let out a bark of laughter, running a hand through his hair. "Wow, you are something, Kate. I can see why my brother is infatuated."

"I think you are reading way too much into this night out between me and your brother." She laughed nervously, taking a swig of her beer as she looked out over the crowd. She didn't belong here among these people. She didn't know why Luke had brought her here, but it was not because he wanted to spend time with her. He wanted to teach her a lesson. That had to be it.

"I beg to differ," Josh said quietly, dangling his beer bottle by his long fingers. "If he wasn't interested he would have written you off during your first meeting with him. How did you meet anyway?"

"I hit his car with mine," she responded, realizing that in every instance she had hit Luke with something.

"Not the Lambo." Josh's eyes widened even more at the thought.

"No, the BMW. I was late for a meeting and he was in my way. Little did I know that he was the one I was in a hurry to see."

"I see," Josh said, shaking his head. "At any rate, my brother is interested. Just remind me to park well away from you and to wear a cup when you play pool."

"Oh god, it sounds worse when you say it," Kate groaned. She was a walking disaster when it came to Luke Wilder.

"I'm joking, kinda. I will give you the inside scoop, Kate. My brother is like our father, ruthless and has the need to succeed like twenty-four seven. I'm a good mix between our two parents, but my need is different. I need to dominate."

"So are you going to turn into a domination-driven man like Christian Grey then?" Kate asked, a smile hovering on her lips. She liked Josh, but she craved Luke. The zing wasn't there when Josh winked or grinned at her like it was with one look from Luke. Some girl who could tie this man down was going to have her hands full indeed.

"Maybe," Josh grinned then stood, setting his empty bottle on the table. "Come, Kate, my dear. I do believe they are playing our song."

"Oh no, I don't dance," she protested as he grabbed her hand and pulled her out of the chair. She had two left feet and the horrible need to step on toes when she even considered dancing.

"Tonight you do. That will get Luke's attention faster than you flew here on his jet. Trust me, Kate. You want my brother's attention, right? Let me prod the beast."

"Don't do anything that will make us look like fools," she muttered as she allowed him to lead her to the dance floor where a few other couples were elegantly dancing to the soft piano music. Josh swung her around and clasped his hand in hers, the other settling lightly on her waist. "See, the way to my brother's heart is to make him feel like he has lost some of the control," he said as he leaned in. "Luke likes to be in control, but you have to show him that you can dominate him as well. I'm sure you gave him hell for the accident, didn't you?"

"I, well, maybe," she answered as he swung them around the floor. So that was the secret? She had to knock him off his pedestal? Somehow she didn't think that was going to be as easy as Josh was making it out to be.

"See, what did I tell you? It doesn't take long being in the black sheep's arms before he comes sniffing. Yo Luke, I see that you finally found us."

Kate nervously turned to find an angry Luke before her, his eyes shooting daggers at his brother. "Kate, I see that you have met Josh."

"I rescued her from the bowels of boredom," Josh said before Kate could force out anything, giving her a wink. "Did you know that she's a beer girl too, Luke? How are your balls by the way?"

Kate groaned as Luke's face reddened slightly, but he didn't respond, instead he turned his intense gold-flecked gaze back toward her. "May I cut in?"

Josh gave her waist a squeeze before letting go; stepping aside for Luke to take his place. Kate swallowed hard as she felt the burn of his hand on her waist, the way his fingers curled around hers as they settled back into the sway of the music. Yes, there was no doubt that Luke was the one who made her heart go pitter-patter. "I'm sorry, I …"

"No, I'm sorry," Luke sighed, some of the tension in his shoulders loosening. "I all but abandoned you as soon as we walked through the door. All of these people are people who we have grown up around, who have been key players in my father's success, and I got lost." He then gave her a lopsided grin, one that warmed her blood. "You probably thought I did it on purpose, as payback."

"I might have," she said slowly, remembering Josh's words. She wasn't going to make this easy for him tonight. "The question is how are you going to make it up to me?"

Luke's eyes widened and Kate silently congratulated herself on the comeback. He stopped their movement and kept their hands clasped together as he tugged her off the floor and to the table where her wrap and purse sat with his brother. His stride was very determined and Kate found herself intrigued at the thought of what was going to happen next.

"Take her to Serendipity, Luke," Josh remarked as he handed her the stuff he had been guarding. "Better yet get her a greasy pie and a couple of beers. She really likes beers. Very nice to meet you, Kate."

"You too, Josh," she smiled as Luke tugged her toward the exit.

\*\*\*

Kate settled into her seat and fastened her seatbelt, a contented sigh escaping her lips as she looked at the man seated across from her. Tonight had gone from the worst night of her life to the best and she had Luke to thank for all of that. He had apparently decided to take his brother's advice and took her out for greasy pizza and cheap beers before they strolled through Times Square for an hour much to Kate's delight. It had been magical, experiencing sights and sounds that she had never thought she would experience, and now their night was coming to an end. The pilot had just announced they would be descending shortly and Kate couldn't help but feel a bit disappointed. "I really had a great time tonight," she said softly, giving Luke a small smile. "Thank you for taking the time to show me some of the city."

"You're welcome," he responded, rubbing a hand over his face. Luke had been a bit distant since they had left the ballroom and his brother. Kate had picked up on the tension that Josh had caused with his interference. She was grateful, of course, for it helped her understand the brooding man before her just a little bit more but the man before her now was the same man she had experienced in the office and she didn't like it. The plane bumped along and soon they were saying goodbye to Lewis and walking back to the car in silence. Kate didn't know what to say as they approached the car but Josh's voice kept running through her mind. Did she dare take the initiative to see where his actual feelings for her, if any, lay? What if he rejected her?

Luke pulled up the passenger side door and turned to look at Kate expectantly. This was it. Kate moved toward him and grabbed his suit coat, pulling herself toward him as she pressed her lips against his. The intensity was immediate. She felt his surprise and then the dominance as his hands reached up to frame her face, his lips going from non-existent participation to seeking in an instant. Kate found herself swallowed by the heat from his touch, the way he demanded entrance into her mouth and when she gasped, he swept in. Their tongues touched and Kate's knees weakened, her hands clutching his jacket tightly to stay upright. Finally he pulled away and laid his forehead against hers, his breath harsh. "Why did you kiss me, Kate?"

"I really don't know," she gasped. "It seemed like a good idea at the time."

Luke laughed then, a long tortured laugh that drove right into Kate's soul. What if he was trying to figure out how to let her down gently? What if she had made some colossal mistake?

Luke pulled away and dropped his hands from her face, the gold flecks in his dark eyes glittering. Kate realized that she had a death grip on his jacket and dropped her hands as well, resisting the urge to run away. She would take her punishment and then cry into a tub of ice cream later.

"Ah, Kate, you are something else. What are you doing tomorrow night?"

Her eyes flew to meet his and she found a lopsided grin on his handsome face. "I um, I have to work at the bar tomorrow night." Ugh, real life was going to ruin it. "But I'm free the night after that." It would be Sunday and the bar was closed so she didn't have to work any shifts. She usually spent the day making up soaps and candles to replenish her inventory, but if she could spend it with him instead, well that would be a pretty good reason to hold off.

"Get in, Kate."

Her mind whirling, Kate climbed in the car and Luke had her home before she could even blink. As usual, her parents' house was ablaze with lights and had been ever since she had started dating back when she was sixteen. No doubt her father was pretending to wait up, dozing in his recliner. He had still continued the routine when she worked late nights at the bar and it was kind of nice to know that someone cared enough to make sure she got home safe. It also meant no "boys" were getting in no matter how old Kate was.

Suddenly shy, Kate glanced over to see Luke looking at her. "Good night, Luke."

"Not yet," Luke said before his lips descended on hers once more, more urgent than their first kiss had been. Kate moaned low in her throat as he nipped at her lips, his tongue doing some pretty wonderful things inside her mouth that left her panting for more. It had been so long. Luke touched her cheek, his eyes searching hers. "Now it's a good night, Kate."

# Chapter 6

"You are crazy, you know that? He's hot, Kate, and rich! I mean any girl would kill for at least those two elements. He took you to New York for Pete's sake!"

Kate rolled her eyes and dried another glass. "Yes, so he is hot and rich. What am I doing with someone like that anyway? I'm not cut out for this, Lilia."

Lilia slapped the bar with her towel as she turned to her friend. "Come on, Kate. It's obvious the man likes you. Why not just see where it goes from here? If you don't, someone else will. It's time to move on from John, sweetie. Way past time."

"This has nothing to do with John," Kate grumbled. "I just, I just don't want to get hurt again, okay?"

"Kate Hensley, you have to jump sometime. What better way than with Luke? He's gorgeous, rich, and totally into you. If you don't want him I will take him."

Kate tamped down the ugly rush of jealousy at the thought of her best friend dating Luke and sighed. Maybe Lilia was right. Maybe Luke was really into her. Most would have run after the pool game fiasco and definitely not take her to NYC like he had last night. Her dreams had been filled with that trip and Luke's kisses, and she woke up feeling very hot and bothered. She couldn't help but wonder if he would keep their date tomorrow, which she was really looking forward to. It wasn't about where they might end up at, it was more about spending time with him. Kate wanted to get to know this man on every level.

"You're right," Kate finally said, admitting defeat. "I need to jump in with both feet."

"Good, I am glad to hear you say that," Lilia grinned, pulling out a folded piece of paper and handing it to her. "Because I wouldn't have given you this otherwise."

"Argh, you are such a bitch sometimes!" she said to her friend as she grabbed the paper and unfolded it, reading the bold script with surprise and excitement. It was a short note from Luke, detailing what he wanted her to bring for their day out tomorrow as well as the ugly early time of 8 a.m. for pickup. A bathing suit? A change of clothes for dining out? Dear Lord, he wanted her in a bathing suit, the absolute worst form of torture for a curvy girl. "When did you get this?"

"I found it stuck to the door this morning," Lilia grinned, smiling like a cat in cream. "I read it but figured it wasn't for me. So what do you think you are going to do tomorrow?"

"I don't know," Kate said, her mouth curving into a smile. "But I can't wait to find out."

\*\*\*

Kate smoothed down her dress that was serving as her bathing suit cover as she threw open the front door, startling Luke as he was preparing to knock. "Hi."

"Hi," he said, his lips curving into a grin. "I take it you are going to attempt to avoid your mother again?"

"Not if you don't hurry," she grimaced, shutting the door behind her and hurrying him down the sidewalk. "Dad has her distracted currently." Thank god. Her mother was primed and ready with the camera this morning. His gleaming BMW sat in her parents' driveway and Kate couldn't help but laugh as they walked around to the passenger side door, the paint unmarred. "So I didn't do any damage?"

"I got it fixed," Luke responded as he shut the door. Kate bit the side of her cheek to keep from grinning like an idiot as he climbed in and they zoomed out of the driveway and down the road. It was promising to be a beautiful day in Haper and Kate couldn't help but wonder where they were going and what they were going to do. It apparently involved water and dinner. When Luke turned toward the airport again, she couldn't contain her excitement any longer. "We are going to fly again?"

Luke parked the car and turned to face her, his eyes sparkling in mischief. "What do you think about a beach in Florida for the day?"

"F-florida?" she stammered, thinking back to when she had shared with him that she had never been able to travel outside of her hometown. Was he trying to prove a point or something? Her inner person was screaming yes while her conscience was telling her that it was too much. Heck, NYC had been too much. "Listen, Luke, you don't have to keep doing this."

"You're right," he sighed, reaching out to gently grip her chin with his fingers. "But I want to. I want you to experience things, Kate. I want you to experience them with me." He then let go and climbed out of the car while Kate tried to process his words. Oh my. Grabbing her stuff, Kate scrambled out of the car and followed Luke to the plane where Lewis greeted her warmly.

"Ms. Hensley, good to see you again."

"You too, Lewis," she smiled as he helped her up the stairs. Luke was waiting in the cabin, a smile on his handsome face. Kate dropped her bag onto the chair and walked up to him, taking his face in her hands. She saw the surprise in his eyes as she gently kissed him on the lips, the warmth of his skin warming her hands. Kate hadn't realized how much she had been looking forward to seeing him today, but having him before her, dressed down into a pair of swim trunks and green T-shirt, had her heart pounding and her mind wanting to do something reckless. After her talk with Lilia, Kate realized she needed to take full advantage of this for however long it was going to go on. He even had her business sense stimulated; she was developing a soap that reminded her of his spicy scent. "Hi."

"Hi yourself," he smiled, his arms going around her and pulling her close to him. Kate inwardly sighed as he leaned down to kiss her again, his hands roaming over her back down to the dip in her spine. "I take it you are good with our trip today then?"

"I can't wait," she admitted, giddy with excitement and happiness. Luke brushed his lips over hers again before he released her, motioning toward her chair. Her chair. That was ridiculous but Kate couldn't imagine anyone else sitting in that space right now. She gave him a cheeky grin and strapped herself in as the plane's engines started up. This was going to be fun.

\*\*\*

Kate leaned back in the chair and gave Luke a dazzling smile, feeling horribly content even though she would be sporting the world's worst sunburn in the morning. They had spent nearly all day on the beach, with a cooler between them and nothing but sugary white sand and the crystal-clear water of the

Gulf of Mexico before them. She knew she would never forget this day for as long as she lived. Now they sat at a cozy outdoor restaurant overlooking the water, the sea breeze teasing her curls. The sun was setting over the water and Kate didn't think she had ever seen such a beautiful sunset in her entire life.

"So Kate Hensley, what do you think of the beach?"

"Well, I think I need to sell everything I own and pitch a tent right here," she laughed, looking at Luke. "My entire life savings might buy just one tent."

Luke laughed as well, his expression relaxed and carefree like she was feeling. It was obvious that being away from everything agreed with him, much better than their trip the other night. "Well, anytime you want to visit, my parents have a hotel on the beach a few hours from here. I think I can pull some strings."

"That's good to know," she remarked, then took a sip of her beer. "Why didn't we go there then?"

Luke's easygoing expression clouded a bit and he cleared his throat, fiddling with his utensils on the table. "Josh is there. I didn't want to run into him."

"Oh," Kate said, clearly confused. "I like your brother. He seems like a nice guy."

"I don't want him to take what's mine," Luke growled. Kate just stared at him. What was that supposed to mean? "He's done it before and I don't want to take that chance again."

"I well, I think that's childish," she said, her initial shock dissipating. He could be talking about anything at this point but it sounded like a ridiculous reason in her opinion. "Your brother seems to care for you, Luke."

"So now you are an expert in my family's issues?" he asked harshly, his eyes narrowed and full of emotion. "That's quite interesting since you have only been in my life for less than a week."

"No, you are right," Kate sighed, reaching across the table to touch the back of his hand. "I haven't been involved long. I'm sure once upon a time you two were as thick as thieves."

"Once," Luke replied, staring at their touching hands with a frown on his face. "We did everything together. Then I got serious and well, Josh didn't. He wanted to race and that was his life. I didn't agree that should be the course of a future career and we fought. He slept with my girlfriend that night."

"Well, she wasn't worth it to begin with," Kate said softly, feeling the hurt and anger radiating off him. Luke looked up sharply and she sucked in a breath at the hurt in his eyes. He must have really cared for her. Oh, the inkling of him caring for her that much was breath-stealing. That was what she wanted, from him.

Luke cleared his throat and Kate removed her hand as their food was delivered and they started to eat silently.

"So explain to me what made you want to make soaps for a living?"

Surprised, Kate laid down her fork and took a swallow of her water this time. They hadn't even mentioned anything about the deal or about the future of her business since their initial meeting. She was starting to believe that he had forgotten the real reason they had met. "It was my grandmother really. She had made her own soaps for years as did her mother before that. I went to stay with her one summer and learned all about soap making. I've done some experimenting since then and launched my online shop a few years ago."

"Now I get the pioneer creation name," Luke said as he cut into his steak, referring to the name of the business that Kate had created. "So it's a family affair then?"

"I guess you could look at it like that," Kate shrugged. "My grandmother made me promise to never sell her recipe. I don't plan to, just the finished product."

Luke was silent for a moment and Kate wondered what he was processing about her business. Was he thinking she was crazy and that her product stunk or was he considering her proposal?

"I gave some of your samples to friends of mine. They all agreed they liked it. I will discuss the possibility of stocking it at the resort with my father."

"Seriously?" Kate asked.

"Seriously," Luke said, a hint of a smile hovering on his lips. "Your product is good, Kate. I think it's worth a trial run at the resort."

"Oh my god, I don't know what to say," she breathed. He could have given her a million dollars and it wouldn't replicate the feelings she had right now. She wanted to launch herself across the table and kiss every inch of his handsome face to show her appreciation but in the end she found herself a bit teary, dabbing the corners of her eyes with the napkin.

"I didn't mean to make you cry."

"I'm sorry," she said, blinking a few times to clear her eyes. "It's just my dream for this product has been to move to the next level and I can't believe it's finally going to happen."

"Well, finish eating and we will get you back to good ole Haper. You have a lot of work to do to get ready for the opening of the resort," Luke grinned, pointing to her food.

Kate giggled and resumed eating, feeling triumphant that she had finally got herself in position to obtain her goal with Pioneer Creations. She had done it.

\*\*\*

The next few days were complete and utter exhaustion for Kate. When not covering at Coyotes and helping Lilia out, she focused her attention on churning out soap and candles like a madwoman, trying to prepare for the opening of the resort. She wanted to have enough for at least the first couple of months and hopefully with the money that she would make, she could take some time out to experiment with new flavors. The one based on Luke's scent was done and she couldn't wait to give him a sample if she could find him. Their trip to Florida had ended with some hot and heavy kissing but since he had dropped her off that night at her parents' doorstep, she hadn't seen or heard from her rich boy.

Sighing, Kate wiped down the bar and threw the rag into the bucket, glad that the shift was almost over. Lilia had gone home an hour ago after Kate had offered to close up shop, intending to finish the books so she would be one step ahead for tomorrow. The doorbell tinkled and Kate turned toward the door, her words dying on her tongue as she took in the familiar face. "I was just about to tell you we are closed."

"So you are going to kick me out?" Luke grinned, closing the door behind him and pulling down the shade on the door that had a closed sign attached to it.

"Well, it depends," she said wryly, leaning over the bar top with her chin propped up on her hands. "What are you offering?"

"Damn, it's good to see you, Kate," he said walking toward her, his expression heated, causing Kate's blood to start to hum in anticipation.

"I missed you, Luke."

He stopped dead in his tracks and Kate wanted to pull the words back in. It was true, she had missed him something terrible. His expression softened and he beckoned for her with one finger. "Come here, Kate."

Swallowing hard, Kate stepped from behind the bar and stopped before him, wishing she was wearing something a bit sexier than the T-shirt with the bar name scrolled across it and some comfortable worn jeans wet in places from cleaning up. Her hair was in a messy ponytail and Kate could only imagine what her makeup looked like. Luke on the other hand looked good enough to eat with his open at the collar dress shirt and grey slacks, his dark hair raked back on his head. He also looked tired and Kate's heart shifted just a little. Throwing caution to the wind, she moved the last few feet to him and wrapped her arms around his waist. "You look like you are about to fall down."

Luke's laugh came out choked as his arms went around her, pulling her until their bodies were meeting each crevice from shoulder to thigh. "It's been a trying week. I would much rather be jet-setting with you."

Kate's heart dipped as she pressed her cheek against his chest, the warmth of his body seeping through the silky layer of his shirt. "We do have to make a living somehow."

Luke pulled back and Kate looked up at him, seeing the humor in his glowing eyes. "You are correct but the latter is so much more fun."

Kate laughed, delight in her voice as Luke leaned down until their foreheads touched, his breath warm. "Kiss me, Luke."

His mouth invaded hers just as she got the words out, his tongue parting her lips and sweeping in. There was intensity in his kiss, desperation to explore every inch of her mouth and Kate felt herself melting in his embrace. His hand trailed down her spine and she shivered, her own hands exploring his muscular back. "You have me on fire, Kate," he mumbled against her lips as he walked them backwards, the wood of the bar meeting Kate's back. Kate gasped as Luke's lips trailed over her jaw, then to her ear, where a sensitive spot had her tingling all over. Her common sense flew out of the window as his hand dragged over her stomach and up the side of her breast before cupping it through her T-shirt. "Tell me you want this, Kate. Tell me you are on fire like me."

"Luke," she said raggedly, her own hands dragging over his shoulders and down the front of his shirt, popping a few buttons so she could feel his bare skin under her fingers. He hissed and she smiled, tugging at the shirt with her hands. Kate knew this was craziness, this lust that seemed to go much deeper than she had ever experienced with anyone. She should stop this, make him take her to his house and finish it but the thought of breaking contact now was not an option. It was just the two of them, in a dark bar, with the rest of the world on the outside.

Luke pulled the shirt over his head and Kate sighed, her fingers running over his perfectly sculpted chest in wonderment. "You're beautiful," she said reverently, placing a kiss over his heart lightly. His breath turned ragged as her fingers played with the sparse hair on his chest before tracing it to the belted waistband of his pants, her own breath coming in short gasps.

"Let me see you, Kate."

This was it. He was either going to appreciate what he saw or run the other way in terror. Biting her lip, Kate dropped her hand and pushed at him lightly to give her some room. Grabbing the bottom of her T-shirt she pulled it over her head before she could change her mind, wishing she had worn a sexier bra at least as she shed that as well. The chill of the AC had her standing at attention and she resisted the urge to cover herself as she met his gaze.

"God, Kate, you are beautiful," Luke swallowed as he reached for her. All of a sudden his hands were everywhere, on her skin, cupping her breasts as he lavished them with his tongue. Kate threw her head back in rapture. She could feel the heat of his mouth on her nipple, the swirl of his tongue as he lazily drew a circle around it. Her head was swimming with desire and her hands reached out, blindly attacking his belt with her fingers. She didn't care what she looked like now, she wanted him all of him and the hell with everything else. He must have sensed her urgency and with a chuckle helped her shed his pants and boxers, the sight of his arousal taking her breath away. "Do you like what you see, Kate?"

"I can't imagine anything better," she said huskily, reaching for her own jeans. His sharp intake told her he approved and she shimmied her pants down, her boldness growing as she stood before him clad in her black lace panties. Thank god she had decent underwear on.

Luke reached out and ran a finger up the crease, rubbing it between his thumb and his forefinger as

Kate's knees buckled. It had been way too long. "I want you, Kate."

"I-I want you too," she admitted, her mind going blank as he reached for her. How were they going to do this? Luke answered it for her, spinning her around until her aching breasts rasped against the bar top, spilling out onto the surface. His hand appreciatively ran over her ass before he pushed her now soaked panties aside, his finger teasing her briefly. Kate felt the contact and gasped, hearing the sound of a condom being torn open before he thrust into her, filling her to the very core. She arched and he gripped her hips, thrusting again and again until the tension of her own orgasm took over and she fell apart. Luke groaned and his thrusts became rapid as Kate struggled to stay upright, the sound of their flesh meeting and separating echoing through the empty space. Luke stiffened and then shouted harshly before collapsing on her back. Kate placed her head on the bar top and fought the urge to laugh, thinking of how grossed out Lilia would be if she knew that her best friend had just had sex in her place of business. It had been thrilling, it had been earth-shattering and Kate felt like she was a renewed woman because of it. She felt Luke kiss her shoulder softly before separating from her, his hand sweeping across her ass before he stepped away. Kate forced her shaky legs to move as well as she gathered her clothes, not wanting to see his face. She had been wanton and now the afterglow of sex brought on a new wealth of feelings that she didn't want to experience.

"Kate." Biting her lip, Kate turned around, holding her clothes in front of her protectively. Luke was looking at her with a hooded expression, his pants now back into their original place. "Are you finished here?"

She didn't know if he meant with their sex fest or what she had to do to close the bar up but she nodded anyway, not trusting her own voice. Why did it have to be so awkward after mind-blowing sex?

"Good," he said with a wolfish grin. "Come on, you are coming home with me tonight."

\*\*\*

Kate stretched her arms over her head and looked up at the ceiling, a stupid grin on her face. She knew it was sometime in the pre-dawn hours and her body felt wonderfully sore from the activities she had experienced in the last couple of hours. This was crazy. Looking over, she noticed that Luke was watching her, an unreadable expression on his face. His hand was stroking her stomach and after what they had just done, there was nothing she had to be ashamed about him doing so. He made her feel beautiful, desirable, and so all-out special that he had nearly brought tears to her eyes when he had reverently worshipped her body. "What time is it?"

she asked softly, reaching out to brush the hair off his forehead.

"Sometime before five," he answered, his voice rough. "I have a meeting in about an hour or so."

"You can't call in to work?" she joked as he captured her hand and kissed the palm of it. She didn't want to leave this massive bed for fear of what the daylight might bring. This was solidifying the fact that they were involved, no more tiptoeing around the sexual tension that had been building from the moment that they had met. Now a whole new worry set in and Kate wasn't sure how she was going to handle it. She was rapidly falling in love with the man next to her and as crazy as it sounded, in her heart it was happening.

"I wish I could," Luke responded, shifting to pull her against him. "I would love nothing more to have you in every room in this house, Kate. I can't get enough of you."

Kate smothered a giggle as she felt his arousal pressed against her bare bottom, resisting the urge to wiggle against it just to see how he would react. His arm draped over her and she sighed in contentment. She wanted nothing more than to pull the covers over their head and live in a cocoon away from the harsh reality of the world. This was the life, she just didn't know how long it was going to last.

# Chapter 7

Kate knew she had a stupid, shit-eating grin on her face but she couldn't help it. She was so damned happy. She maneuvered her car into a parking spot in front of Wilder Corporation and killed the engine, looking in the rearview mirror at her reflection. It was funny what awesome sex did to a person. Everything on her was damn glowing. It was all because of her hot-blooded millionaire who had kissed her senseless before she had left his house this morning. This was all very unexpected and her mind was still reeling from the fact that she was falling in love with a man way out of her league.

Sighing, Kate grabbed the bag on the passenger seat and climbed out of the car, nervousness setting in. She was taking a huge risk dropping in on Luke like this but she wanted to show him the product she had been working on, the one that she had created from his scent. It was named Green Envy though there was nothing green about it.

Kate took the elevator to the second floor and pasted a smile on her face as she stepped out, seeing the same receptionist seated at her desk. She would love to go up to her and announce that she was here to see her boyfriend, but she didn't. Kate didn't know if she was really classified as the girlfriend yet but she desperately wanted the position of girlfriend if he was willing to give it to her. "I'm here to see Mr. Wilder, Luke Wilder."

The receptionist gave her the eye but waved her back. "Mr. Wilder is in a meeting currently, Ms. Hensley. He has *ordered* me to let you come on back to his office if you so happen to ever come by."

"How nice of him," Kate smiled sweetly, giving her a little wave just to irritate her further. Okay, so this had to be something, right? He was declaring to at least his secretary that she was something to him. With a little hop in her step, Kate walked back to his office, finding it empty. It was sleek and dominating, just as he was, and she couldn't help but run her finger over the glass desk. Wouldn't it be fun to mess up this desk just a bit, him included of course? Gah, her breath was short just thinking about seeing him in his suit behind that desk right before, well, she messed him up in her own little way.

"Kate."

Turning around, Kate found the object of her fantasies staring back at her, a tall, leggy blonde beside him with a smug look on her face. "What are you doing here?"

"I came to show you my new products," she said slowly, not liking the look that the blonde was giving her. "Did I catch you at a bad time?"

"Why, Luke, you didn't tell me you had the small-town businesses in your back pocket! How quaint."

"Nicole, enough," Luke growled, not taking his eyes off Kate. Kate on the other hand didn't want to take her eyes off the woman who was touching her man with her red-tipped nails like she owned him. Where had this vicious spurt of jealousy come from?

"What? I was just saying that perhaps we could use some of the local things at our wedding, of course, you know, to make nice with the locals."

"Did you just say wedding?" Kate burst out, all the blood draining from her face. She looked over at Luke and caught him running a hand over his face wearily, but not outright denying the fact that he was engaged. Oh god, she had let down her boundaries and got screwed again.

"Yes, Luke and I are engaged. Our families are old friends and we practically grew up together. Hoteliers and beauty essentials tend to go hand in hand, isn't that right, Luke?"

"Kate, we need to talk," Luke interrupted, shaking off Nicole's hand on his shoulder. His eyes were imploring her to look at him, to not panic, but Kate was far beyond that. She was pissed.

"Oh well, let me congratulate you on your engagement then," she said, her voice dripping with disdain as she picked up the now worthless bag of soaps that had held so much promise. "I'm sure you will have a happy life together."

"Kate, don't," Luke said as she passed by, reaching out to touch her arm. Kate shook it off angrily, the hurt in her body becoming almost too much to bear. She wasn't going to show him that he had devastated her. "I have nothing else to say to you. Please lose my number and don't even think about stepping one foot in the bar. Have a nice life." She then brushed past him and with blurry eyes, made it to her car before the tirade of emotions overtook her.

"Damn you, Luke! Damn you!" she screamed as she slapped her steering wheel with her palm, big, fat tears rolling down her face. How could he do something like this to her? How could she trust him totally and fall in love with him thinking that he was one of the good guys? She should have known better, she should have known that no guy like that would actually fall in love with a girl like her. It had been too good to be true and she was left picking up the pieces yet again.

"Never again," she vowed, wiping her tears with the back of her hand. She would rather be alone for the rest of her life than go through this all-consuming hurt ripping her heart out.

\*\*\*

*"Kate, I need to explain what is going on. Dammit, Kate, please pick up the phone."*

Kate pressed end on the voicemail and resisted the urge to throw her phone across the room lest she break the damn thing. It wasn't like she could afford a replacement now that it was obvious her future was all but over. With a sigh she laid it on the nightstand and pulled the covers over her face, wishing that she could just disappear. It had been a week since the debacle at Luke's office and while it was the most gut-wrenching, heart-destroying memory of her life, way worse than John's could have ever been, she was kind of glad it had happened. The last thing she would have wanted was to fall madly in love with him and realize that she was the other woman in his life, not the main one. Her mind said that she was smart, that he was good for nothing and to be glad that it was all over. Her heart, however, said that something wasn't right and she should return his call, at least allow him the chance to explain before Kate dumped his ass all over again. She was torn at what to do about this and horribly so.

Rubbing a hand over her face, Kate forced herself to leave the bed. Tonight was her shift at the bar and while she wanted nothing more than to wallow in her self-pity and think of a million ways to gut Luke Wilder, she couldn't let down her best friend. It wasn't in her nature. So even with a heavy heart Kate took a shower and got dressed, avoiding her parents as she crept out of the house and into her car. She knew she wasn't hiding anything from them. Her mother could spot an issue a mile away but the less they knew, the better it was going to be. Their daughter had failed once again to spot a loser.

With a long, frustrated sigh Kate drove to the bar, hoping that Lilia would not bring the whole situation with Luke up before they worked. A best friend's intuition had brought Lilia over with a pint of ice cream and plenty of tissues the other night. Kate had told her everything. Lilia had left a Luke hater as well so Kate did not have to worry about her best friend trying to patch them back together. Maybe the hustle and bustle of the bar would keep her mind off things for at least one night.

Pulling into a parking spot, Kate climbed out of her car and wearily opened the door.

"Hi Kate."

"Josh?" Kate asked, startled to see Luke's brother lounging against the bar with Lilia behind it, staring at him like he was a fallen angel. "W-what are you doing here?"

"I came to see you," he grinned, flashing his teeth. "I've been getting to know your friend here."

"He's an ass," Lilia muttered, slapping the towel on the bar. "I can see how he's related to Luke." Kate was surprised to see Lilia's reaction to loveable Josh and filed it away for a future conversation. There was very little that rattled her friend, but apparently Josh had touched a nerve. "I'm going to the back to stock. Just remember we open in an hour."

"Okay," Kate answered though she could see that the jab was directed at Josh and not her. "Do you want to sit, Josh?"

Josh ambled over to the nearby table and pulled out a chair, gesturing for Kate to sit before he took a seat as well. Kate couldn't get over the fact that jet-setting Josh was here in Haper with no other reason but to see her. She doubted Luke had called in his brother, considering their relationship, so her curiosity was piqued as to what he knew. He looked as hot as ever, dressed casually in a buttoned-down shirt that wasn't tucked into his jeans and sporting that grin that looked so much like Luke's that Kate's heart hurt with every beat. Even with the deception, she missed Luke like she would miss one of her own limbs. The devastation was deep and all the way to her soul. She doubted she would ever truly heal. John's betrayal had hurt badly, but Luke's betrayal was killing her. "So, spit it out. Why are you here?"

"It's good to see you, Kate," he laughed, leaning back in the chair. "You look a hell of a lot better than my brother does."

"I knew you were here because of him," she fumed, pushing her chair away from the table. "You can tell him to go to hell, Josh. Don't leave out the hell part, okay?"

"Whoa, wait, he doesn't know I am here," Josh interrupted as Kate started to stand. "I swear it, Kate. He doesn't know I am talking to you or he would probably kill me. Please, sit down. I would like to talk with you."

Kate eyed him with the biggest stink eye she could muster as she lowered herself back down in the seat, crossing her arms over her chest. "Fine. What are you here for then?"

Josh sighed and ran a hand through his hair, looking weary. "You know you are perfect for him, right? All of the women in his past relationships, they have bent to his will, allowing him to dictate their lives but you are different, Kate. You are actually the challenge he can't seem to conquer."

"I'm a person, you know, not a challenge," she grumbled. "And he seems to be just as equally good at screwing me over for that, that blonde."

"Nicole is a bitch," Josh forced out, a sour look on his handsome face. "She thinks she rules the roost in Luke's life but that ship sailed long time ago."

"Before or after you slept with her?" Kate countered, putting two and two together. She remembered Luke's-words about his ex-girlfriend and she hoped to god that he hadn't left a string of broken engagements across the country.

"See? You are brilliant," Josh laughed harshly, rubbing a hand over his face. "Yes, I slept with Nicole if you want to call it that. I was so trashed that night and really don't remember a whole lot. Honestly, I really don't think I even did the deed, but you really can't defend yourself when a naked woman is lying in your bed and your brother just happens to walk in."

"Well, I can understand," Kate said, a whisper of hurt in her voice as she remembered how she felt seeing another woman draped all over Luke. It had been heartbreaking.

"Listen, Luke is crazy about you," Josh said, leaning on his elbows on the table before him. "I know my brother. He wouldn't be sticking around this place, no offense, if he wasn't intrigued with something and that something is you, Kate. I personally have insight that he has officially bought the townhouse, which he wouldn't have done if he weren't planning on staying for an extended period of time. Why do you think that is?"

"He's got the resort," she muttered.

Josh laughed, his eyes twinkling as he shook his head. "Not so much. My brother can move wherever the hell he wants and still maintain the responsibilities of the resort. I'm telling you he's found something worth settling down for and that is you, Kate, whether you believe it or not."

"What about this fiancée of his then?" she countered, tamping down the small flicker of hope in her chest. "He can't fake that she exists and thinks that they are going to get married."

"Nicole was that person once upon a time but she isn't any longer. She loves to throw that up when it benefits her and no doubt she saw you as a threat."

"Yeah right," Kate laughed then, looking down at her body "Are you serious? I'm no threat to her. Hell, I can't even fit into her biggest T-shirt."

"You have his heart," Josh said softly, reaching across to pat Kate's hand. "Honey, you are the biggest threat to her because she knows she has lost Luke forever."

Kate sniffed as the tears pooled in her eyes, thinking about how much she loved the dolt. She did of course love him but the thought of how gut-wrenching it would be to lose him—that made her physically sick.

What if he decided that he really didn't want her anymore? What if Luke saw someone else he wanted more? She was being so stupid, but these were real fears, real thoughts.

"I'm not saying to run right back into his arms," Josh continued, withdrawing his hand and standing. "He was an ass not to clarify the mistake immediately but hey, we are guys and only human. I mean he's probably been blowing up your phone since then, correct?" Kate nodded and Josh grinned. "Bingo. Give him another chance, Kate. It might be the worst idea you ever come up with but at least you will know you tried. Don't leave it like this."

Walking over, he brushed his lips over her cheek, the unusual scent of grease and salt air filling her senses. "And dammit, be part of our screwed-up family in the process, will you? I like you, Kate."

She laughed as he exited the bar, then looked down at her shaking hands. Josh had a point. She just didn't have that same knowing feeling like she had with John when she had caught him cheating. There was that nagging sensation that maybe, just maybe Luke hadn't lied but her pride was holding her back. Did she dare reach out and grab that brass ring again? Did she dare lay her heart on the line and wait for the outcome? Could she live without Luke?

# Chapter 8

*Two weeks later*

"Come on, Kate! Quit looking in the damn mirror and step out of the car. At this rate, they will have already torn down the damned resort."

Kate squared her shoulders and climbed out of Lilia's car, straightening her short black cocktail dress as she looked up at the illuminated resort before her. When the glossy invitation had come, she had been surprised and intrigued, wondering why she had been invited to such a black-tie affair. The invitation had also given her a plus one to accompany her and there was no one else that Kate wanted at her side tonight other than her best friend. She had been so busy with the orders that were piling in from her Etsy account all of a sudden, spending much of her time pushing out products left and right. The invitation had given her some time to think about her future as well.

"Geez, come on, slowpoke!" Lilia urged as she tugged on Kate's arm. "I bet they have free food and booze and I am certainly not going to miss out on that."

"Well, I hope it was worth you shutting down the bar tonight," Kate remarked as they walked under the beautiful pergola to the entrance of the resort's main building. The sweet smell of jasmine filled the cool night air, the last dying sign of summer on the horizon. Changes were coming and Kate wasn't just thinking about the weather. Inside the lobby was gorgeous, the plush seating and muted colors of greens and blues reminding Kate of the ocean. A waiter passed by, handing them both a flute of champagne and directing them to the ballroom/conference center.

"This is gorgeous!" Lilia exclaimed as they made their way to the ballroom. "Just think of all the money that will be rolling through our town and the bar. Hell, you might want to consider setting up a storefront, Kate. I bet you would make a killing."

"Maybe," Kate replied as they passed by the small but elegant gift shop. A square of green caught her eye and she stopped in her tracks, nearly causing Lilia to run over her. No way. That couldn't be.

"Oh my god, that's your soap, Kate!"

Dumbfounded, Kate walked into the shop, her heart thudding in her ears as she saw a complete and utterly beautiful display of her soaps smack dab in the middle of the shop, her insignia plain as day on the sign above the table. "I don't understand."

"Hello, my name is Mary. Can I interest you in trying out one of our signature soaps tonight? You will find them stocked in every room at our resort."

"What?" Kate asked the girl, who was looking at her like she had just grown two heads. "Did you say every room?"

"Y-yes ma'am," she replied, taking a step back. "And the candles are in our lobby, ballroom, and spa."

"Huh, that explains your sudden Etsy orders," Lilia remarked as she peered over Kate's shoulder. "You have got to go find him. If that isn't a declaration of love, I don't know what is."

Kate turned to her friend and grinned, her heart lighter than it had been over the past couple of weeks. "You're right. I have to go find him now."

"Hell, go then! What are you waiting for?" Lilia grinned, pushing her to the door. Kate hurried down the hall to the ballroom, giddy with excitement. He had done this. Luke had done the one thing she had hoped for and dreamed of. He hadn't forgotten about his promise and he sure as hell hadn't given up on their relationship. She was starting to wonder when his texts and messages had stopped bombarding her cell phone about the time her Etsy shop had really taken off. "You silly, silly man," she breathed coming to the ballroom door.

Kate stepped inside and scanned the room full of people, hoping and praying that she wasn't too late. He was over by the open French doors, his hands in his pockets and a pensive look on his face. Kate stopped and admired him for a moment, her heart doing double time. He was so damned handsome and he was all hers if she wanted it to be. She would have to be a fool not to. Straightening her dress, Kate walked over to him. "Hello Luke."

He turned and she saw the relief in his eyes, his face impassive. "Kate. I'm glad you came."

"Thank you for the invite," she said politely though she wanted to throw herself at him. She would play nice for now. "This place is gorgeous. You did a good job."

"You are gorgeous," he said, giving her a once-over, his eyes now full of the desire that was running through her veins. "Did you stop by the gift shop? We have a lovely array of soaps."

"Why?" she asked hesitantly, gripping her hands together in an effort not to touch him. "Why did you do it, Luke?"

"These past weeks have been hell without you," he said harshly, running a hand through his hair nervously. "God, Kate, I have missed you so damned much."

"Why did you do it?" she repeated, her throat dry. If he didn't say it, it didn't matter, not now.

"Hell, Kate, I love you, isn't that obvious?"

Kate's face broke out into a smile as she launched herself at him, savoring his touch as he slid his arms around her waist, his face buried in the curve of her neck. "I love you! I've missed you so much, Luke. You have no idea."

He nearly crushed her against him, his lips kissing the sensitive spot behind her ear. "I think I have a pretty good idea, babe."

She then pulled back, fiddling with his bow tie nervously. "So do you have a free room in this joint?"

"Hell yes," he said, releasing her only to grab her hand instead, pulling her through a startled crowd. Kate only giggled as he led her through the hall and to the elevator, where he jabbed at the button impatiently. "Damn the elevators."

"Luke," she said, tugging him toward her before he destroyed the button. "Kiss me."

He gave her a sad smile as he framed her face with his hands, his eyes searching hers. "I never meant to hurt you, Kate. I am so damned sorry for that."

"It's over," she said softly, wrapping her arms around his waist. Luke nodded and pressed a gentle kiss on her lips, so gentle that it brought tears to Kate's eyes. This was the man she loved. She could feel it radiating off him in waves and she had never felt so cherished in her entire life. "Wait, why didn't you just ask for the soaps? I still would have sold them to you."

"I wanted to show you that I meant business about the resort and about us," Luke replied, nibbling at her lower lip. "Besides, I wanted to keep you busy. You probably wouldn't have sold them to me otherwise."

"You are probably right," she laughed as the elevator doors opened. Luke grabbed her hand once more and they stepped in, the doors barely shutting before he had her in his arms once more, nuzzling her neck. "Have you ever done it in an elevator before, Kate?"

Kate smiled as she reached over and pulled the emergency stop, the elevator shuddering to a stop. "How about you show me how it's done, Mr. Wilder?"

\*\*\*

*A month later*

"Kate! Dammit, I can't find my own ass in all these boxes!"

Kate laughed as she watched Luke wander into the bedroom, a frown on his face as he surveyed the mess she had created. "Lord, woman, how much stuff do you really have at your parents' house? Please tell me this is all of your belongings now."

"It was your idea for me to move in here," she chided, pushing herself off the floor. Her parents had just delivered some things she had stored in their basement and she had been going through the boxes to sort out what she wasn't going to need anymore. "You could have just moved in at my parents' place, you know."

"No, I don't know," he muttered as she came toward him. "That wasn't even funny, Kate. Did you really just take over my office too?"

"I remember you losing that space in a game of strip pool, sir," she smiled, pointing a finger in his chest.

"I remember other things about that game too," he grinned, wrapping his arms around her and nipping at her nose. "I think I deserve a rematch at least."

Kate laughed as she wrapped her arms around him and laid her head on his chest, feeling the steady beat of his heart under her cheek. God, she had never been so happy before. Luke had wasted no time moving her into his place after their reunion at the resort and the last month had been pure bliss. She still was working on her soaps, but her time at the bar was over. Luke had set Lilia up with a competent accountant and while she hated ditching her friend and leaving her high and dry, Kate had realized that it was time to focus on her own career. Lilia had understood of course, for she was a businesswoman herself.

"Hey, aren't we having dinner with your parents tonight?" Luke mumbled against her hair. "I distinctly remember not being able to turn your mother down."

"We are," Kate sighed, pulling out of his arms and looking around at the mess she had created. "Thank god we are going to their house." She then smiled and pulled her shirt over her head, enjoying the hiss that followed. "I guess I better start getting ready."

"I'll join you," Luke replied thickly as Kate wiggled out of the yoga pants she had been wearing as she moved toward the master bathroom. "Do you think they will care if we're late?"

# What to read next?

If you liked this book, you will also like *The Stolen Bride*. Another interesting book is *The Race for Love*.

# The Stolen Bride

Lindsey Thomas is at the top of her game. With a successful career, fabulous friends and Patrick Crawford, her wonderful fiancé, her life is just where she wants it. That is, until Patrick dumps her the night of their engagement party. Brokenhearted, Lindsey heads to her best friend Kate's family beach house to heal, as it is temporarily vacant and she hopes some alone time at the beach will help her feel better. But when Kate's brother, novelist Harris Welling, shows up unexpectedly, things get complicated. Harris insists that she stay at the house as he is only there to get some work done before the rest of the family arrives the following week, and Lindsey agrees, despite her reservations. Lindsey soon finds herself drawn to her best friend's handsome older brother. So soon after her disastrous breakup, she tries her best to resist the growing chemistry between them, but she cannot deny her feelings and a relationship quickly develops. However, when Patrick pops back into her life unexpectedly wanting to be with her again, she is forced to make a choice ... but will she make the right one?

# The Race for Love

Lilia Anderson needs help and fast. The bar she has worked so hard to make successful is in danger of being stolen out from under her by her own uncle, and she needs a significant amount of money to save it. One meeting with an infuriating man from her past, Josh Wilder, has her partnering with the handsome auto racer to raise the money. She tries to keep her heart protected, but soon Lilia finds that she is looking forward to his calls, visits and even his races. Just when Lilia loses her heart to Josh, he gets into a horrible accident and she sees a side of him that gives their relationship an unexpected twist.

# About Olivia West

Olivia West is a bestselling romance author who is known for her captivating stories with interesting characters, unusual settings, adventurous plots and intriguing relationships. In each of her stories she tries to make readers see in their imagination a mental movie in which they can feel emotions of the characters and are curious about what will happen next.

# One Last Thing...

If you believe that *Taming the Billionaire* is worth sharing, would you spend a minute to let your friends know about it?

If this book lets them have a great time, they will be enormously grateful to you – as will I.

Olivia

www.OliviaWestBooks.com

Made in the USA
Las Vegas, NV
22 February 2022

44370663R00062